our
generation®

This is Audrey-Ann's story.

# AUDREY-ANN®

# THE DRESS
# IN THE WINDOW

BY

SUSAN CAPPADONIA LOVE

ILLUSTRATED BY TRISH ROUELLE

*An* Our Generation® *book*

MAISON JOSEPH BATTAT LTD. *Publisher*

*A very special thanks to the editor,*
*Joanne Burke Casey.*

Our Generation® Books is a registered trademark of Maison Joseph Battat Ltd.
Text copyright © 2010, 2011, 2012 by Susan Love
ISBN: 978-0-9844904-8-6
Printed in China

*To Mom and Dad,*
*who always make Christmas memorable.*

Read all the adventures in the
**Our Generation®** Book Series

*One Smart Cookie*
featuring Hally™

*Blizzard on Moose Mountain*
featuring Katelyn™

*Stars in Your Eyes*
featuring Sydney Lee™

*The Note in the Piano*
featuring Mary Lyn™

*The Mystery of the Vanishing Coin*
featuring Eva®

*Adventures at Shelby Stables*
featuring Lily Anna®

*The Sweet Shoppe Mystery*
featuring Jenny™

*The Jumpstart Squad*
featuring Juliet™

*The Dress in the Window*
featuring Audrey-Ann®

*The Jukebox Babysitters*
featuring Ashley-Rose™

*In the Limelight*
featuring Evelyn™

*The Most Fantabulous Pajama Party Ever*
featuring Willow™

Read more about **Our Generation®** books and dolls online:
www.ogdolls.com

# CONTENTS

**EXTRA! EXTRA! READ ALL ABOUT IT!**
*Big words, wacky words, powerful words, funny words...
what do they all mean? They are marked with this symbol \*.
Look them up in the Glossary at the end of this book.*

# Chapter One

## LOVE AT FIRST SIGHT

My feet wouldn't budge. It was as if I were glued to the sidewalk.

"C'mon, Audrey-Ann," my best friend Mollie said. "We're going to be late for school."

"Let's go-o-o-o-o, slowpoke!" my little brother Jerry said, as he tugged on my puffy, polka-dotted vest. Then, deciding I wasn't going to move anytime soon, he shrugged and raced off to catch up with our mom, Mollie, and Mollie's younger sisters.

I stood in front of the Kids Emporium and stared at the display inside the window.

An emporium is a store that sells all different kinds of things. This one sells everything kids like—toys, clothes, pretty headbands, colorful notebooks, cute pencils, games, beaded necklaces, glow-in-the-dark stars—you name it.

Every day when the six of us walk to school, we pass right by the Kids Emporium. It always has interesting displays in the windows.

For example, last summer the window was bright with beach balls, swimsuits, goggles and flippers. When it was almost time for kids to return to Button Cove Elementary School in August, there were lunch boxes and backpacks in all the colors of the rainbow.

But I'd never seen anything like *this* window display. I couldn't take my eyes off it.

The dress in the window was the most beautiful dress I'd *ever* seen—and I do mean ever. Fancy. Frilly. *Fantastically gorgeous.*

In my mind, I could see myself wearing it to the Christmas Celebration, the biggest and best school party of the year. I imagined the way the ruffles would float around me when I danced. How soft the satin would feel. And that the dress would be the prettiest one at the party.

*It's perfect for the Christmas Celebration,* I thought. *Absolutely perfect!*

"Close your mouth or you're going to catch flies," Jerry teased me. "Mom said we have to scoot, skedaddle, vamoose—in other words, get going! School starts in eleven minutes!"

Eleven minutes! I snapped back to reality* and was surprised to see my reflection in the Kids Emporium window. My jaw hung down and my eyes were open wide. Seeing myself with that weird expression made me giggle.

There was no time to waste if I wanted to be sitting at my desk when the teacher started roll call. As I began skipping to the corner, I took one more quick look over my shoulder at the dress. I caught up with everyone just as the crossing guard gave us the OK to go.

"What were you looking at?" asked Mollie.

I was panting so much from sprinting, I could hardly speak. "Mollie (huff-huff) I found (huff-huff) the dress (huff-huff) of my dreams!" Then I told her every little detail about the light-catching, crinkled-satin design with layers of ruffles in the prettiest green ever.

"Wait until you see it!" I gushed. "There's even a matching purse!"

From behind me, I heard a familiar voice. It was Betsy, a girl in our class.

"Are you talking about the party dress that's in the Kids Emporium window?" she asked excitedly. "I just love it!"

*Oh no, is she thinking about buying the dress, too?* I wondered. I could feel my heart beating like crazy. Ba-*boom*! Ba-*boom*! Ba-*boom*! Ba-*boom*!

# Chapter Two

## DODGEBALL DRAMA

The dress in the window popped into my head about 50 times at school that day.

*I'll ask Mom if we can buy it,* I thought, as we played dodgeball in the gym at recess. *Maybe we can go after school.*

Bam! A big red rubber ball hit me on my right shoulder and practically knocked me over. Ouch!

Who threw the ball and got me out? It was none other than Betsy, who was pumping her arms overhead in victory and dancing around in a circle.

Never mind the fact that I wasn't paying attention when the ball bounced off my body. It seemed to me that Betsy tried to outdo me every chance she had.

I slunk over to the sidelines rubbing my sore muscles and had plenty of time to think about it.

Last year Betsy and I both competed for the part of Royal Princess in the school play. She got the part and I got stuck being the head and front legs in a donkey costume. She got to sing a solo*. I got one measly line: "Hee-*haw*, hee-*haw*!"

Then there was the time Betsy beat me in the spelling bee and came in first in the Jump-for-Joy Jump Roping Contest—all in one day!

I suspected that Betsy even had her eye on my leaf-raking job. While I was raking the Martinsons' yard one day, I found a soggy yellow flier under a mound of leaves. The wind must have blown it out of their mailbox. It advertised:

**Betsy & Brothers Raking Service**
Fast & Friendly
Leaves Bagged & Carried to the Curb

How could I ever compete with Betsy and her two football-playing brothers?

I was determined to rake every inch of the Martinsons' yard really fast and be extra friendly. I made sure every last leaf in the yard was bagged. What a workout!

Mr. Martinson was so impressed with my work he hired me on the spot to rake each week at the same time. It was the best job a nine-year-old could have—I got to be outside in the crisp fall air and bring my dog, Ginger, to work with me, too.

The only drawback to living across the street from my

job was Jerry. He'd wait until I'd gathered a huge pile of leaves, then gleefully run up and do a "cannonball" in it. Then Ginger would leap in, too, and they'd roll around a few times.

"Jerry, look what you did to my pile," I'd complain. "It's scattered all over the place."

"LEAF it to me to make a mess," he joked.

I groaned, then grinned. Bad jokes and all, it's impossible to stay mad at Jerry. He's such a charmer. Plus I have to admit that I finally gave in and did a few cannonballs myself.

But that was two months ago, way back in October. I gazed out the gym window and saw snowflakes coming down fast and thick.

*Almost time for Christmas*, I thought. *And for the Celebration. And for me to wear the dress in the window. That will be my chance to outshine Betsy for once.*

✿ ❧

My teacher, Mr. Skippington, was wearing his crocodile-patterned tie. He wore plain tan pants and a boring white shirt with a collar every day, but his ties always had pizzazz*.

16

There must have been a hundred ties in his closet, printed with basketballs, playing cards, music notes, pink flamingos, flags from around the world, dolphins, jigsaw puzzle pieces and more. Some ties were funny (like the one with polar bears on ice skates) and some had holiday patterns (valentine hearts, Easter eggs, groundhogs and birthday cakes).

"OK class," said Mr. Skippington, "it's nearly time for the school bell to ring—and you know what that means."

"Snowball fight!" chimed in one of the kids in class.

"Sledding!" I said.

"I meant *homework*!" Mr. Skippington exclaimed. "But before you go, I have a couple of important announcements."

As was his usual habit, he straightened his tie and cleared his throat (ahem!). I don't even think he knows he does this, but everyone in class does. It means: "Is everybody paying attention?"

Betsy was in the front row. She stopped whispering to the girl next to her and sat straight up in her chair, listening to Mr. Skippington.

"The school is holding the first-ever Christmas Poetry Contest," he said. "Poems are to be written about 'What

17

Christmas Means to Me.' This is perfect timing because we are learning how to write poems right now."

I glanced quickly at Mollie and we both perked up. This news sounded exciting.

"If you'd like to enter a poem in the contest," Mr. Skippington said, "and I hope you will, please turn it in within two weeks."

*Fantastic!* I thought. *I love to write.*

"And as you all know," he continued, "the Christmas Celebration is coming up. We're looking for girls and boys to volunteer to be part of the Decorating Committee.

"That would mean using your creativity to give the Christmas Celebration a festive* look. We'll also need volunteers to help make the decorations and put them up the day before the event.

"Would anyone like to volunteer for the committee? The first meeting is on Thursday."

My hand went up like a rocket. I jiggled it around to get Mr. Skippington's attention. "I'll volunteer for the committee!" I exclaimed.

"Me too!" said Mollie.

"Me three!" said Betsy.

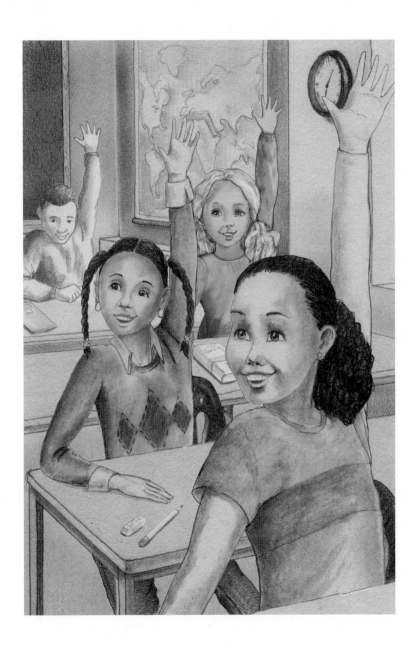

## Chapter Three

## FIDDLE WINKINS

It was a good thing that I had worn my boots that morning. About six inches of snow had fallen while we were in school. It was a fun walk home with Mollie's mother, who said you got to make a wish for every snowflake you caught on your tongue.

When Jerry and I got home, my mom was busy shoveling our driveway. "I made you both apples with peanut butter for a snack," she hollered over the roar of the snowplow that was driving by.

"Go ahead and eat, then please come outside and start shoveling Mrs. Maple's driveway." Then my mom added, "And that means you, too, Jerry."

Jerry shoveling? Jerry goofing around was more like it. He'd be no help at all.

"Do we have to?" I pleaded. It was a very short driveway, but still...

My mom stuck her shovel in the snow, took off her

gloves and wiped away the snowflakes that were clinging to her eyebrows. "Now Audrey-Ann, you know Mrs. Maple is older and can't get around as well anymore. Be a good next-door neighbor and help out."

"But Mom…" I groaned.

"Mrs. Maple took you for long walks in your stroller when you were a baby. She read you books and pushed you on the swing. She put bandages on your boo-boos when you scraped your knees learning to ride your bike. Now you can be kind to her like she has always been to you."

I looked down at the ground. In my heart, I knew she was right. But shoveling? Now? Ugh! I trudged up the front steps.

❦ ❦

As I shoveled, Jerry hurled snowballs at me. For a seven-year-old, he has great aim. One snowball hit me on the collar of my vest, slid onto my neck and melted all the way down the inside of my shirt.

Putting my shovel down, I brushed the snow off my vest. *I look like a snowman*, I thought.

I noticed the world of white around me. It was a

winter wonderland. A blanket of light, fluffy snow covered the earth and sparkled as if it was sprinkled with glitter.

The falling snowflakes gave me an idea for a craft project. When I went inside I'd fold pieces of white paper and cut them into snowflakes. Then I'd....

The loud slam of a door interrupted my thoughts. Mollie came bounding out of her house a few doors away and up Mrs. Maple's driveway. Her eyes were bright and excited. "My mom said she'd take us snowboarding in a few minutes. Go ask your mom."

Looking at Mrs. Maple's driveway, which was nearly knee-deep in snow, I was angry with myself for dilly-dallying* in the house earlier. I could easily have been done shoveling by now. "Sorry, Mollie, but I can't," I said.

Disappointment was written all over her face.

"Hey, Mollie," shouted Jerry as he started pelting snowballs at her, "we're having a BALL!"

The snowball war began. It was us against him and somehow he won.

We flopped down and made snow angels, doing windshield-wiper motions with our arms and legs to make the angels' wings and skirts.

22

About ten minutes later, Mollie's mom and sisters picked her up in their car to head to the ski area. I grabbed my shovel and continued clearing the driveway.

To pass the time, I thought about the Poetry Contest. *What does Christmas mean to me?* I wondered.

*Hmmmmm…it means stringing colorful lights on the tree. Decorating cutout Christmas cookies. Singing at the annual\* holiday party with my*

*Grandma Gertie, aunts, uncles and cousins. And getting all dressed up and taking pictures. Aha!*

*I'll write about the dress! I'll name the poem "The Perfect Christmas Dress,"* I decided.

By the time I had shoveled my way from the end of the driveway to Mrs. Maple's back door, Jerry had made a snow fort as tall as himself.

"We are SNOW lucky!" he shouted. "Come and sit in my castle."

I tried to scowl, but couldn't help smiling.

Something moving in the window caught my attention. It was Mrs. Maple pulling back the lacy curtains and peeking out the window. With her crooked pointer finger, she jabbed the air toward a patch I'd missed on the side of the driveway. I nodded and went to clear the area.

As I threw the last shovelful onto the snowbank, Mrs. Maple knocked on the window and motioned for Jerry and me to come in. My mom, who was still shoveling, gave us the thumbs-up sign that it was fine to go inside and visit.

Jerry and I took off our boots at the door and stepped into the entrance. We sat on wood chairs like we had done for years. I couldn't put my finger on it, but something was missing.

I didn't remember Mrs. Maple being that fragile* or that small. I guess I had grown a lot since I'd seen her in the fall.

For someone who was going nowhere, she was all dressed up. Her hair, which was as white as the snow outside, was done in soft curls. She was wearing a fancy blouse that matched the color of her blue eyes, pearly blue earrings, a matching necklace and peach-colored lipstick.

Mrs. Maple chattered away, asking questions about school and talking about her son who lives here in Button Cove.

It was like old times. Ever since I can remember, when we visited Mrs. Maple we sat around her kitchen table. Then she usually offered us a special treat: her home-baked chocolate chip cookies. That was what was missing—the smell of freshly baked cookies.

Ever so s-l-o-w-l-y she made her way to the kitchen counter. She reached for her cookie jar, lifted the lid and offered us a cookie. Jerry dipped his hand in and then I did, too.

The thought of Mrs. Maple's cookies made my mouth water. I was in for a surprise. The minute that my thumb and finger touched a cookie, I knew it wasn't homemade.

I took a bite. That was the second surprise. Instead of a scrumptious, sweet cookie, it was stale. There was no crunch to it. And the taste was...well, like nothing at all. No flavor.

Without even looking at Jerry, I could sense the expression on his face. We both took tiny nibbles of our cookies to be polite. Neither of us wanted to hurt Mrs. Maple's feelings.

When she turned to put the cookie jar back on the counter, I put what was left of my cookie in my pocket and Jerry quietly spit what he'd stored inside his cheek into a napkin. He made a sour face and tried to hand the napkin to me, but I swatted his hand away.

After that, Mrs. Maple asked us if we'd like to play Fiddle Winkins.

"Fiddle Winkins?" Jerry and I both asked at once.

"You've never heard of Fiddle Winkins?" she said, pretending she was surprised. "Oh it's fun. I'll show you how."

She explained to us that it was similar to miniature golf, but you use an orange instead of a golf ball, and objects from around the house to create the course. Our golf clubs were a curved umbrella handle, the rounded end of a cane and a broom.

The person with the least amount of strokes* at the end would be the Fiddle Winkins champion.

We looked around the house for things the orange could go over, under and through. The first hole was in the living room.

The orange wobbled along, never going in a straight line. It was tricky to get the orange to go between the legs of the piano stool, through a tunnel (a big cookbook we stood in an upside down "V"), around a circle of spoons, over a ramp made from a cardboard box and into the hole (a pan that was set on its side).

Thinking up the course was as fun as playing the game.

At 5:15 p.m., when we were on the sixth hole, the phone rang.

It was my mom calling to say that dinner was ready and we should head home. We wished we could stay and finish the Fiddle Winkins game, but we all agreed to play again after the next snowstorm.

All the fresh air and shoveling had made me hungry. My mom's cooking smelled extra wonderful when I walked through the front door.

"Did you have a nice visit with Mrs. Maple?" she asked.

"A blast!" I exclaimed.

"But those cookies!" whispered Jerry, as if Mrs. Maple might hear him across our two yards. "They were so old they must have been made when George

Washington was president!"

"Oh Jerry," I teased, "that's the way they are supposed to taste." I winked at my mom to get her to play along.

"Huh?" said Jerry, with a confused look on his face.

He was falling for it. I could tell. "Those are magic cookies," I said seriously. "Didn't you know that?"

"That's right," said my mom. "Their dull, stale taste brings to life all the interesting, fresh facts in your brain. Now you'll ace* your science test tomorrow."

"No way," he said, with an expression that showed he might just believe us.

"Speaking of magic," I began, "I saw the most magical, beautiful, gorgeous Christmas dress in the window at the Kids Emporium today. Mom, can you please, please, pretty-please-with-sugar-on-top buy it for me?"

My mom stopped mashing the sweet potatoes and looked up. "Audrey-Ann, we just bought you an absolutely lovely dress for Thanksgiving. You just had to have it, remember?"

"Yes, but this one is dazzling! Glamorous! Sensational!" I said.

Mom talked softly, which is what she does when she wants to let me down easy. "I'm sure it is, but you already have a dress. I have an idea—you still have the money you saved up from raking the Martinsons' yard in the fall, right? If you want the dress, why don't you use that money to buy it?"

"I already have plans for that money," I complained.

"Here's another idea. If you want a new dress to wear, why don't you wear Mollie's blue velvet dress and she can wear your Thanksgiving dress?"

"Mollie's dress is really pretty, but I have my heart set on the dress in the window, Mom. The Christmas Celebration is two weeks away. I could wear it then. You'll fall in love with it when you see it!"

"I'm sure I would love it, honey, but we can't just buy another party dress when you have a perfectly good one."

"Not even for our big Christmas Eve party at Grandma Gertie's?" I begged.

"I'm afraid not," Mom said.

30

I stewed* in my bedroom, feeling disappointed and frustrated. I put on my Santa hat to cheer myself up.

Doing something with my hands always makes me feel better. I remembered the idea I had earlier for the snowflake decorations, so I got out a stack of white paper. I folded a piece and snipped out tiny shapes, then unfolded it to see the lacy snowflake I'd made. But I didn't stop at one. I created a blizzard!

After spreading old newspapers on the floor, I set the snowflakes out in rows, brushed them lightly with glue and sprinkled on glitter. When they were dry, I used string to loop them together in groups of three and four.

My mom got a stepstool and taped the snowflakes to my bedroom ceiling. "I have one word for this," she said. "Amazing."

I was feeling better, but knew I still had a decision to make. I had been saving up my money so I could buy the materials to make gifts. I didn't have enough money for both the craft supplies *and* the dress.

What would I do now? I really wanted that dress!

I could just imagine the look on Betsy's face when I waltzed into the Christmas Celebration wearing it. But I also could imagine the big smiles on my family's faces when they unwrapped my homemade gifts on Christmas morning.

ॐ ॐ

That night in bed, I turned on my side, then my back, then the other side. I fluffed my pillows and clutched my fuzzy rabbit with the floppy ears.

The sheets seemed bunched up around my feet so I smoothed them out. For some reason my pajamas felt scratchy. And the click-click-click noise from the heater was annoying, although it had never bothered me before.

I couldn't get comfortable.

Most of all, I guess I couldn't get comfortable with the question in my mind: Should I buy the dress, or buy the supplies for the gifts?

# Chapter Four
## WHAT'S THE BIG IDEA?

Before class the next day, I showed Mollie an idea that I'd found in a magazine. It was step-by-step instructions for making a penguin out of a soda bottle that was covered in a white sock. Its flippers were black felt and the top hat was a laundry detergent cap.

"He's so cute!" Mollie gushed, pointing at the picture. "Awwww, he even has a little striped scarf."

"At the committee meeting today," I told her, "I'm going to suggest that we make these for the tables at the Christmas Celebration."

Betsy was turned around in her desk looking at us. When our eyes met, she quickly glanced* away. Was she snooping around to hear our conversation?

I snapped the magazine closed just as Mr.

Skippington adjusted his lucky tie patterned with four-leaf clovers.

"Ahem!" he said, clearing his throat. "While I'm passing back your poetry homework, would anyone like to read theirs aloud?"

He was making his way down the first row and handing the poems back to the students. As he handed Betsy's back to her he said, "Well done, Betsy!"

"Thank you, Mr. Skippington," she said. "I'd like to read my poem."

I caught a glimpse* of a large red "A" at the top of her paper. A golden star gleamed next to it.

*Is there anything that Betsy isn't good at?* I thought.

Betsy scooted out of her chair and walked up to the front of the classroom to read her poem. Her voice was nice and loud, but I didn't hear one word.

I was too busy looking at my own poem which Mr. Skippington had just handed back to me. It said: "Nice start. Still needs work."

"For your next poetry homework," he said to the

class, "please write about your family's Christmas traditions."

Mollie raised her hand. "What exactly *is* a tradition?" she asked Mr. Skippington.

"A tradition is an event that's been done for a long time and becomes the usual thing you do," he said. "For example, on your birthday, you might get to pick whatever you want for dinner. That's one example of a tradition. Or, on Christmas Eve, you might leave a plate of cookies for Santa and carrots for his reindeer next to your fireplace. That's a tradition, too."

❧ ❧

Mr. Skippington had told us that there are two good ways to improve our poetry: 1) to practice, and 2) to read other people's poetry.

If I wanted to get my poem picked for the contest, I was going to have to practice. And read. Then practice more. And read more.

During study time, I asked the school librarian if she could help me find books of poetry. She seemed tickled*. Hopping out from behind her desk, she

36

started trotting past the storybooks, around the reading tables and alongside tall bookcases. I had to jog to keep up.

"This is my favorite section in the whole library," the librarian said in a low voice, as if she was telling me a secret.

She spread her hands wide to show me five rows of shelves filled with poetry books. I selected an armful, sat in a comfy chair and plunked them down next to me.

The first book I read was of poetry about the seashore. Reading the poems reminded me of all the things I loved about the beach. Hearing the sound of the waves. Wiggling my toes in the warm sand. And watching the funny birds with their long skinny legs skitter* up and down the shore.

One book was filled with poems about sports. And another was about nature.

The last book was silly. I laughed out loud at the poem titled, "The Toad That Tap-Danced to Texas." The librarian helped me make a copy of it for Mollie.

"Welcome Decorating Committee members!" the assistant principal, Ms. Russo, said to us on Thursday.

"Thank you in advance for volunteering your time and creativity to make the Christmas Celebration special. We have a lot to do to make the gym festive."

I was excited to be on the committee—give me paper, scissors, paint, glue and markers, and I'm as happy as can be.

"First, let's make a list of decorations that we'll need," Ms. Russo continued. She wrote our ideas on the blackboard:

<u>We'll need decorations for the:</u>
Stage
Walls
Dining Tables
Buffet\* Tables
Christmas Tree
Ceiling (to hang)
Gym Doors

"Now let's put our imaginations to work," said Ms. Russo. "I hope you all brought your ideas."

Betsy raised her hand. "I have an idea," she said.

My cheeks felt hot. I had a bad feeling.

"Yes, Betsy. What's your idea?" Ms. Russo asked.

"I saw something cute in a magazine that would be great for centerpieces*," she began. "It's a penguin that you make out of a soda bottle, a white sock and felt. Cotton puffs give the look of snow. It's so adorable."

That was *my* idea! I was astonished*.

"That does sound cute," praised Ms. Russo. "Let's write it down. Any other suggestions?" she asked the group.

One by one the students told their ideas for winter-themed decorations. Mollie suggested Santa faces. Other classmates' ideas were good, too: gingerbread men, candy canes, wrapped gift boxes, poinsettia flowers, snowmen, mistletoe, angels, reindeer, Christmas bells and ice skates.

"That's a good start. We're out of time for today," said Ms. Russo, "but we'll continue at our next meeting."

As we filed out of the room, I muttered* to Mollie, "I can't believe Betsy stole my idea!"

"I don't think Betsy would do that, Audrey-Ann," Mollie said. "I bet Betsy saw the same magazine that you did."

I'd expected that Mollie would agree with me. I didn't know what to say.

"She was snowboarding yesterday," Mollie continued, "and we rode the chairlift together. She's actually a really nice person when you get to know her."

*Now* I didn't know what to *think* either!

# Chapter Five

## CREATIVITY IN PROGRESS

Friday was a snow day—hooray—that meant no school! Unfortunately it also meant shoveling. Once again my mom shoveled our driveway, while Jerry and I went to shovel Mrs. Maple's driveway.

Of course, Jerry didn't really help, but that was OK because instead he made a giant snowman that faced Mrs. Maple's kitchen window. He put my dad's straw hat and plaid scarf on him.

"Isn't this great!" Jerry said as he gave the snowman a great big goofy grin. "There's no business like SNOW business!"

Next he began making a snow woman. I knew from years of playing outside together, he'd soon have a whole family of snow people lined up in Mrs. Maple's yard.

*I'll take a break and help Jerry make a snow baby*, I decided.

When Mrs. Maple pulled back the curtains to check how my shoveling was going, I saw her smile. She used her hand to make a scooping motion toward her. That was her signal to us to come inside.

"No faces about the cookie this time," I said to Jerry as we stomped our feet on the porch to get the snow off of our boots.

"Are you kidding?" he said. "I got an 'A' on my science test. I'm going to eat every bite."

Mrs. Maple, Jerry and I played Fiddle Winkins

again and I laughed so hard I had tears in my eyes. We used every room on her first floor except for her crafts room, which had a sign on the closed door: "Creativity In Progress. Do Not Enter."

When Mrs. Maple said she couldn't play another round of Fiddle Winkins, I wondered why.

She must have read my mind. "I'm working on an important project that I have to get back to," she said. "I can't get around like I used to, but I still like to do things with my hands."

That sounded interesting. I wanted to know more, but Mrs. Maple was in a hurry to hustle us out the door.

∽ ∾

I thought about the dress in the window on and off all weekend. When Mollie and I were painting flowerpots for our teacher's Christmas gifts, it crossed my mind, *is someone trying the dress on right now?*

When I was helping my dad dry the dishes, I worried. *Did Betsy's mother take her to buy the dress today?*

By the time Monday morning rolled around and

we were walking to school, I was all worked up. I hoped that the dress would still be in the window.

Phew! It was. And it was just as beautiful as I remembered it.

*Maybe I can think of other presents I could make with materials in our craft scraps bin,* I thought. Then I wouldn't have to pay for supplies. I didn't really think that was possible, but I'd pretty much made up my mind: *I have to have that dress.*

Later that day at the Decorating Committee meeting, Ms. Russo explained how we'd get everything done.

She said we would work in teams. One team would create the wall decorations, a different team would do table decorations, and so on.

"Also," she explained, "committees usually have someone in charge to organize all the people and activities. That person is called a chairperson.

"Sometimes people share the job. Since we have a lot to organize in a short amount of time, I think it would be good to have two people. Any volunteers?" asked Ms. Russo.

Before she had even finished her sentence, I raised

44

my hand. At the exact same instant, so did someone else: Betsy.

There was no backing out now. We were the only two people with our hands up.

"Excellent," said Ms. Russo. "Betsy and Audrey-Ann, you are the official co-chairpersons of the Decorating Committee.

"For our next meeting, please pick teams and choose what decorations they'll be making. Can you arrange to meet in the next few days to get the ball rolling?"

We both nodded yes, but inside I was thinking, *oh no!*

# Chapter Six

## THAT'S WHAT FRIENDS ARE FOR

Tuesday brought more snow. And more shoveling.

"Why am I responsible for shoveling Mrs. Maple's driveway?" I asked my mom while I was taking off my boots. I shook the snow off my mittens. "Why doesn't her son do it? He lives just a few blocks away."

"He's in California until January for work. You know," she said, "we live too far away from your grandma to shovel her driveway, but a neighbor is helping her out with that. Doesn't it make you feel good to do that for someone else?"

"I suppose. But Mrs. Maple doesn't even leave the house," I said. "So why does her driveway need to be shoveled?"

"Well, for her grocery deliveries, for the mailman, for lots of reasons," she said.

DING-DONG! DING-DONG!

Betsy had agreed to come to my house for the first co-chairpersons meeting. I felt uneasy about it.

"Mmmmm," said Betsy, when I opened the door. "It sure smells good in here. Like a movie theater."

"Oh, thanks," I replied. "My mom made popcorn for us."

We sat down at the kitchen table and I got out a folder of ideas the Decorating Committee had suggested. I'd also added ones I'd clipped out of magazines, copied from library books and my mom had helped me find on the Internet. Betsy emptied her ideas out of a big orange envelope.

We spread all the suggestions out on the table and put them into three piles: "Good," "Better" and "Best." We tried to narrow it down. There were so many decorations we had a hard time choosing.

Pretty soon we were both confused. We certainly couldn't make all 27 kinds of decorations that were in the "Best" pile.

"Here's an idea," said Betsy. "How about if we draw the gym to show how a few of the decorations would go together?"

I got a big sheet of poster board and Betsy started sketching. The walls were crooked and the floor sloped downhill. The tables were teeny-tiny and the chairs were just the right size for giants.

She pointed at her drawing. She threw her head back, put her hand on her stomach and howled with laughter.

It's not very nice to poke* fun at someone else's art, but I couldn't help giggling, too. It was a pretty bad picture.

"Oh boy," Betsy said with a half-sigh and half-laugh. "What was I thinking?" She flipped the poster board over and handed me the pencil. "*You're* the artist. You'll do a *much* better job."

"Me?" I asked.

"You're the best drawer in class," she said, pointing to me.

That made me feel really good.

Little by little we figured out what decorations should go where. The way we had it set up in the picture, the gym looked great. Except...we agreed that it needed a finishing touch. But what? We went through our piles again but nothing seemed just right.

I had a thought. I told Betsy about the hanging snowflakes I'd made.

"I got a little carried away," I admitted. "Come see the snowstorm in my bedroom."

The motion of opening the bedroom door created a breeze that made the dangling snowflakes spin and sparkle like ice crystals.

Betsy took a sharp breath in, then slowly out. "Beautiful, Audrey-Ann. Like I said, *you're* the artist."

We decided to hang hundreds of snowflakes from the gym's ceiling.

Who would have ever thought shoveling would inspire* an idea for decorations?

On Thursday, Betsy announced to the Decorating Committee and Ms. Russo that we had something really special to show them. She said it was all my idea.

"Imagine turning the gym into a winter wonderland indoors," she said, pointing to the strand of glittery snowflakes I held up. The committee ooohed and aaahed.

"We'll need everybody's help making them," I said. "Christmas is all about traditions, so we're asking you to start a new tradition. Please have each person in your family make a snowflake and jot their favorite Christmas tradition on the snowflake."

Betsy continued, "Once they're hung, the gym will be filled with special Christmas memories."

I added, "It's easy. We'll show you how." We passed out scissors and white paper and took everyone through the quick steps to make the snowflakes.

"Here's how the gym will look when it's completely decorated," said Betsy, holding up the poster board I'd sketched.

After that we paired up the committee members into teams of two or three people by drawing names out of a hat. We gave each team a decoration to be in charge of.

"The supplies you'll need to make your decorations will be here for Thursday's meeting," I said. "Thanks for coming."

Mollie patted me on the back when she came up to inspect the drawing I'd done. "This looks fantastic!" she said. "What a party it's going to be!"

"Mom! Mom!" shouted Jerry. He was looking out the dining room window, then sprinted up the stairs to find my mother. "Come quick! There's an ambulance at Mrs. Maple's house!"

"What?!" I rushed to the window and saw a man and a woman in navy blue coats wheeling a stretcher* out of Mrs. Maple's house to the ambulance. I felt frantic. Not knowing what to do, I ran to the door and yanked it open, ready to run out into the snow in my slippers and pajamas.

My dad put a gentle hand on my arm before I got out

the door. "Audrey-Ann, you need to stay here. Your mother will ride with Mrs. Maple to the hospital."

"But what's wrong? Is she going to be OK?" I asked.

My mother grabbed her purse and coat, quickly kissed us goodbye and told us she'd call as soon as she knew anything.

Jerry and I watched as the stretcher was carefully eased into the van. We waved to Mrs. Maple but I don't know if she saw us. All we could make out was her snowy white hair and the blanket that covered her.

I felt helpless. Jerry was still standing in front of the window even though the ambulance carrying Mrs. Maple and my mom had driven out of sight.

"C'mon, kids," said Dad. "How about if you make cards to let Mrs. Maple know you're thinking about her?"

"Poor Mrs. Maple!" Jerry said.

"She has no family to be with her," I added. "Her son is in California."

"We'll call him," my dad said in a reassuring

tone. "In the meantime, she has us. We'll be here for Mrs. Maple, just like she has been there for us so many times."

"I wish I could do something!" I said.

"You already have," my dad said. "If it hadn't been for you, Audrey-Ann, the ambulance wouldn't have been able to get up the driveway to help her."

# Chapter Seven

## KETCHUP & CARROT STICKS

When Jerry and I came downstairs the next morning for breakfast, my dad told us that my mom was sleeping in. She had been at the hospital most of the night.

"Here's a note for you," he said, giving me a sheet of flowery purple paper.

I read it out loud:

Hi Audrey-Ann and Jerry,
Good news! Mrs. Maple is going to be fine. The doctors thought that she might have broken her hip when she slipped on the basement stairs last night.
They did lots of tests. Luckily her hip isn't broken. But they wanted her to stay in the hospital a little longer to make sure she is OK.
The cards you made for Mrs. Maple are really sweet. I'll bring them to her this morning. You can visit her tonight when she comes home.
XOXOXOXO,
Mom

"We have to leave for school in fifteen minutes," Dad said when I'd finished reading. "What should we pack for your lunches and snacks?"

"Ketchup and carrot sticks!" said Jerry.

"Yuck. How can you eat that?" I asked.

"I love ketchup," replied Jerry, pretending to kiss the ketchup bottle.

"OK, OK, time to put on your coats, hats and mittens," Dad said with a laugh. "I'll carry the backpack for the first person who's ready to go."

Jerry leapt up from the table. "KETCHUP with me if you can!" he shouted to me with a grin.

With all that I had on my mind (Mrs. Maple, the Poetry Contest and the decorations), I had forgotten about the dress for a little while. Thankfully it was still in the window that morning. No one had scooped it up—*yet*.

Poems for the contest were supposed to be handed in that coming Tuesday. I'd been thinking about mine every chance I had. I even put together words and rhymes while I was riding in the car, brushing my teeth and petting Ginger.

As Mr. Skippington passed back to us our corrected poems about Christmas traditions, I felt antsy*. I was anxious to see how I did.

He made his way down the rows and I could see that Betsy got an "A" again and another gleaming gold star.

Mr. Skippington handed my poem back to me. A silver star shined right next to a "B+"! He'd written in red: "You put a lot of heart into this! Good job!"

"Who would like to read their poem aloud?" asked my teacher. "Audrey-Ann, would you like to start?"

I felt proud to read my poem to the class. It was about how my family decorates our Christmas tree together. We have over 50 ornaments and each one has a special story. As we put each ornament on the tree, we tell where it came from.

There's a star ornament made out of tinfoil with Jerry's picture in the middle (I made that in kindergarten when he was just two years old). There's a gigantic fake diamond ring that my dad gave to my mom when he asked her to marry him (he's kind of a joker; the real ring was in his pocket). My favorite is a tiny angel whose halo lights up (my grandma gave it to me when I turned six).

It was interesting to hear the traditions that kids in my class celebrate with their families. Some hang stockings on the mantel. Others decorate Christmas cookies.

Our classmate Carol's poem told about how her family makes Letterbanket cakes. Letterbanket cakes are formed into the shape of the first letter of each person's name in her family.

José's poem described how his family makes a piñata together and fills it with tiny presents and sweets. They hang it up at their holiday party, then take turns getting blindfolded and swinging a stick to crack it open.

Charlotte's poem was about how, on Christmas Eve, her brothers and sisters put their shoes by the fireplace. It's their hope that Father Christmas will fill them with presents during the night. Luckily for them, he always does.

Marty's poem told about Christmas caroling with his parents and neighbors. They knock on doors, sing songs and sometimes are invited in for a cookie or hot chocolate.

We were having such a good time reading our poetry, Mr. Skippington said it would be OK, just this once, to postpone* our math lesson so everyone would get a chance to read their poem.

## Chapter Eight
### FROM THE HEART

Mrs. Maple beamed when Jerry and I brought over homemade cookies for her. She said our cards cheered her up.

My mom had told us that Mrs. Maple was still pretty tired and we should only stay a short while.

I noticed that her hair wasn't carefully curled like it usually was and she wasn't wearing her pretty jewelry and peach lipstick.

But she was as chatty as always and told us about the clown that came into her hospital room and made a crown for her by blowing up long balloons and twisting them together.

"I wore it all night," Mrs. Maple said. "After all, it's not often that you get to be a queen for a day."

When she asked us about our plans for Christmas, we told her that we'd travel to our Grandma Gertie's house for Christmas Eve, which is about an hour and a half away. I look forward to it all year long.

Everyone dresses up and we decorate a gingerbread house together. My uncle plays the guitar, one of my cousins plays the piano and my aunt plays the harmonica. We all sing and have the best time.

I told Mrs. Maple that every year I make an ornament for my grandmother and hang it on her tree.

We asked about her plans and she said, "Well, my son will still be away, but I'll do what I usually do—make my family's traditional Christmas Eve dinner and play Christmas songs on my piano."

*Alone on Christmas?* I thought. *What fun would family traditions be if there was no family to share them with?*

Sadness swept over me. Maybe it was because we'd been talking about traditions in class. Although everyone had different traditions, the one thing we all had in common was enjoying them with our families.

"Do you want to hear a Christmas joke?" Jerry

asked, changing the subject. "What does the school in the North Pole teach?"

"I give up," I said.

"Me too," said Mrs. Maple.

"The ELF-abet!" shouted Jerry.

We all laughed. Thank goodness for Jerry's corny jokes.

Maybe it was my imagination but when it was time for us to leave, I thought I saw tears in Mrs. Maple's eyes.

Bright stars were twinkling in the black sky while we walked home. The weather forecast predicted that we'd have a white Christmas. Mrs. Maple was home from the hospital. Everything was good so why did I feel so glum*?

To get me out of being down in the dumps, I decided to go over my poem for the contest one last time. At the top of the page I had written: "What Does Christmas Mean to Me?" Under that I'd written the title: "The Perfect Christmas Dress."

As I read my poem over, a thought was nagging at my brain. The dress in the window *was* beautiful.

But is that *really* what Christmas means to me?

What about baking and decorating cookies with my mom and Jerry? Gift shopping with my dad every year? Hanging ornaments on our holiday tree as a family? Making an ornament for Grandma and hanging it on her tree? And volunteering with my mom to wrap gifts at the local bookstore to raise money for the children's hospital?

I crossed out a line of my poem and replaced it with something from my heart. Then I erased another line and found better words to express my feelings. Finally, I crumpled the poem up and started fresh on a new sheet of lined notebook paper.

By the time my mom reminded me to get ready for bed, I had finished rewriting the poem from the first line to the last, including the title.

The dress in the window was special, but it could never *make* the celebration special. Only being among family and friends can do that.

# Chapter Nine

## WE WISH YOU A MERRY CHRISTMAS

"Jingle bells, jingle bells, jingle all the way, oh what fun…" Mollie, Betsy and I sang along with a radio station that was playing Christmas carols. We were sitting cross-legged on the floor in my living room and snipping white paper with scissors.

The Decorating Committee had brought in tons of snowflakes their families had made, but we still needed a lot more.

Jerry chimed in, "Jingle bells, the batboy smells, robins lay square eggs—"

"Alrighty, Jerry," said my mom, "how about if you come help me make these coconut snowball cupcakes for the Christmas Celebration?"

Jerry was still singing his made-up words to the song as he followed her to the kitchen. Betsy and

Mollie giggled.

Betsy pointed to an ornament on our Christmas tree. "Is that the star that you wrote about in your poem?"

I nodded, took the ornament off the branch and handed it to her. Mollie was humming along to the radio that was now playing, "We Wish You a Merry Christmas."

"Awwww, Jerry is so funny," said Betsy. She was talking about a baby picture of Jerry that I'd pasted in the middle of the ornament. The photo was taken right after Jerry had dumped his little plastic bowl of spaghetti on top of his head.

Jerry burst into the room. Wearing a cooking apron and holding a whisk up to his mouth like a microphone, he sang, "We WHISK you a Merry Christmas, We WHISK you a Merry Christmas...."

I shook my head and smiled.

After we made 60 snowflakes, we were ready for some real snow. We bundled up and went sledding on the hill behind our house.

That afternoon my dad and I were heading out to do our annual Christmas shopping trip together.

Every year I help him pick out my mom's present. I've saved im from many bad gift choices, such as the red lawn mower e was going to buy for her once.

"But red is her favorite color," he said, clearly discouraged hat I was shaking my head no.

Then there was the time I had to remind him that the red irrings he wanted to buy were the same ones he had bought for her the Christmas before. His heart is in the right place though.

Before we left our house, I put all the money from raking leaves into my wallet. It was a hard decision, but I'd decided that making the gifts was more important than wearing the dress.

I unfolded a piece of lined notebook paper. It was a list of craft supplies I needed to make Christmas presents for my mom, dad and brother and an ornament for my grandmother. There were nine items on it. I brought a red pen to check the items off the list as I found them. That way I wouldn't forget anything.

*Mom, Dad, Jerry and Grandma Gertie are going to love these presents*, I thought to myself. *I'm doing the right thing.*

"What's on your list this year?" Dad teased as we walked along. He was digging around for clues about what I was making him for Christmas.

"You know I can't tell you that," I said. "That would ruin your surprise."

As we joked back and forth, I couldn't help but notice the dress in the Kids Emporium window. Even though I'd decided not to get the dress, it still took my breath away.

*Why not try it on*, I thought, *just to see how it looks?* Then worried. *But what if I'm tempted to change my mind and buy it?*

I asked my dad if he'd hold my wallet. "But don't give it to me until we're in the craft store," I said. He agreed.

Breathing deeply, I opened the heavy wood door. The sales clerk behind the counter glanced up when she heard the door bang shut.

I smiled and asked, "May I please try on the dress in the window?"

"Oh, I'm sorry," she replied. "That dress has already been sold. It's being picked up this afternoon. We just haven't gotten around to putting a different dress in the window."

"S-s-s-s-sold?" I couldn't believe my ears. I turned to face the back of the dress and saw the small sign that said, "Sold."

"Yes," the sales clerk said with a frown. Then she added brightly, "Sorry about that…but we have lots of other pretty dresses in the back of the store."

"Thank you," I said, blinking back the tears that were welling up in my eyes. I drifted to the back of the store to act interested.

I didn't understand why I felt like crying. I wasn't even going to buy the dress. But for some reason, I felt disappointed. Terribly, awfully, horribly disappointed.

Dad called to me with excitement in his voice, "Audrey-Ann! I see a red wheelbarrow across the street at the hardware store. Your mother will love it!"

I burst out laughing. That shook me out of the mood I was in about the dress.

We stopped into the sporting goods store and finally decided my mom would like a new tennis racket (it was red!).

Then we went to the craft store where I found the supplies I needed. Craft stores are one of my favorite places to be because they're filled with endless creative possibilities. I had all day Sunday to make my gifts—and I couldn't wait!

# Chapter Ten

## THE A-MAZE-ING DAY

*Will it ever stop snowing?* I wondered as I zipped up my puffy, polka-dotted vest.

Once again, my mom, Jerry and I headed out to shovel. After a few minutes, Jerry tossed his shovel to the side and announced that he was about to make the neighborhood's first snow maze*.

"Admission is 10 cents," he said, "but since you're my sister, I'll let you in for free."

The whole time I shoveled, Jerry dug paths in the deep snow. There were many turns, dead* ends, and a few surprises too (a rubber ducky in a corner and smiley faces drawn on the white walls with a paint brush and cranberry juice). The maze covered almost our entire side yard and was as deep as the snow.

Jerry spotted a few kids and their parents coming up the street. They were on their way to go sledding. "Step right up!" Jerry shouted to them. "It's an a-MAZE-ing experience!"

He showed them where to start and told them you had to crawl through the maze. "No peeking over the walls—that's cheating," he instructed them. "If you come to a dead end, you must turn back around and try another route. When you find your way out of the maze, you earn a lollipop."

The kids crawled in, hollered to each other, squealed and had a grand time trying to find their way out of the maze.

Then they must have told all the kids on the sledding hill how fun it was, because a whole bunch of other people showed up.

Finally I was done shoveling the driveway and scrambled into Jerry's maze. I must say it *was* pretty a-*maze*-ing.

Out of the corner of my eye I saw the curtains move in Mrs. Maple's window. I looked up and saw her motioning with her finger.

*Did I miss a spot?* I thought. Then I did a double take*. *No, she's not pointing, she's inviting us inside.*

Jerry's pocket, half-full with the change he made from the maze, jingled all the way to Mrs. Maple's house.

"Since you did all the shoveling," he said, "we'll split

the maze money."

"Gee, thanks Jerry," I said.

Mrs. Maple held out her cookie jar to me. "Help yourself.'

*Yum*, I thought as I reached into the jar. *I'll bet these are the cookies we made for Mrs. Maple. No stale cookies today.*

My fingers felt around, but all they came across were the cool, smooth sides of the jar and a thin, folded slip of yellow paper.

I grasped the paper and held it up for Mrs. Maple to see. "Um…"

"Oh my, what's that?" asked Mrs. Maple. "What does it say?"

I read the handwriting out loud:

> *I'm all out of cookies—*
> *look for your treat under the Christmas tree.*

Confused, I looked at Mrs. Maple to see if she could explain this strange paper. She had a twinkle in her blue eyes.

"Go ahead then," she said. "Do as the paper says."

I got up but still didn't quite get it. I poked my head into the living room. Under Mrs. Maple's Christmas tree was a large flat box wrapped in blue paper. A tag read: "To One Super

74

Shoveler. Thank You From Mrs. Maple."

"Open it, open it!" cheered Jerry.

I looked at Mrs. Maple, who pretended she had no idea what it could be. "I guess you'd better get to the bottom of this mystery and unwrap it," she said.

I love surprises! I wanted to make this surprise last, but I also wanted to rip the paper off the box and find out what was inside. I carefully peeled the tape from one end, then, not able to wait any longer, I tore off the blue paper and lifted the top of the cardboard box.

Inside was an absolutely, positively beautiful dress—in my size—that was every bit as magical as the dress in the window.

Fancy. Frilly. *Fantastically gorgeous.*

It was green satin and velvet with red satin roses and bows, plus a matching purse.

"Close your mouth or you're going to catch flies," joked Jerry to me.

I was shocked. I knew Mrs. Maple had once been a fashion designer. "You made this for me?" I asked her.

"While you were shoveling, I was sewing," said Mrs. Maple proudly. "Do you like it?"

"I love it!" I gave Mrs. Maple a hug, but not too tight because she was still sore from her fall.

"I'm going to wear it to the Christmas Celebration this weekend!" I said, holding the dress up to me and twirling around and around.

# Chapter Eleven

## LET THE CELEBRATION BEGIN!

My jaw hurt from smiling for so long.

"Just one more," my mom promised, clicking the camera for what seemed like the millionth time.

"Mom, I think we'd better get going so I'm not late for the Christmas Celebration," I said, skimming my hands across the shimmering green dress Mrs. Maple had made. It fit me just right.

"One last photo…tilt your head up, move to the left, just a little more to the left…"

I could see I might grow old standing there smiling. My mom likes to get oodles* of photos from every angle, for every occasion or no occasion at all.

While she snapped pictures I thought about the busy, wonderful week I'd had.

I'd spent almost all day Sunday making gifts. They turned out even better than I'd hoped. I was so excited for my family to open their presents on Christmas morning!

I made a Hot Chocolate Mix for my dad and bought a mug to go with it.

It was fun making the candleholder for my mom. I cut a Christmas ornament out of red tissue paper, pasted it on the red glass holder and added a green candle. To make it look extra fancy, I painted the plain base shimmering gold.

I knew Jerry would go crazy over the gift I made for him: a "Breakfast In Bed Coupon." He always wants to eat in his room but it's strictly against our house rules. I ran it by my mom and she said since it's a gift, she'll make n exception* to the rule.

The ornament for my Grandma was different from any 'd ever made for her. It was a heart made of red felt with vhite stitching.

I thought about how on Tuesday, I'd turned in my poem or the contest. Then on Thursday, Mr. Skippington had ;iven me a bright blue envelope.

*What's this?* I wondered, as I tore open the envelope.

I unfolded the piece of lined notebook paper inside. It was ny poem for the contest. Written across the top in red letters t said, "Congratulations, Audrey-Ann! You are a winner of he Poetry Contest!"

All my practice and reading had paid off. Imagine. Me, a amous poet. I was going to read my poem on the stage at the Christmas Celebration.

And Betsy would be reading hers, too. During our lunch )reak, Mollie and I made a "congratulations" card with a hooting star on it for her.

To top off the already fantastic week, the Decorating Committee worked together on Friday to decorate the gym.

The stage at one end of the gym was festively decorated vith red and silver helium* balloons. They were bundled like bouquets behind a microphone. Round tables and buffet tables were arranged at the other end of the room. The center of the gym was empty so everyone could play holiday games there.

Mollie and Carol made the most delicious Christmas tree centerpieces (yes, delicious centerpieces!) for the tables.

First they covered Styrofoam™ cones in double-stick tape, then stuck green-and-white peppermint candies in clear wrappers all over them. The finishing touch was a star on top.

The tablecloths were made of big sheets of plain white paper. We cut sponges into star shapes, dipped them into red and silver paint and stamped stars all over the tablecloths.

Striped candy canes and gingerbread men, made of painted paper, were displayed on the walls. The janitor hung our snowflakes from the ceiling. Wow, did they sparkle!

∽✿ ✿∾

The last photo my mom took was of Mrs. Maple and me in her kitchen. She fussed a little with the bows on my dress to make them just right and spun me around so she could see how I looked.

"You're the prettiest poet I've ever known," she announced.

"Don't forget," my mom said to Mrs. Maple as we headed out the door, "you're coming to our house on Christmas Day for dinner, right?"

"I wouldn't miss it for the world!" Mrs. Maple said, then added to me with a wink, "And afterwards, we'll teach your parents how to play Fiddle Winkins."

As we drove to the Christmas Celebration, I started getting butterflies* in my stomach thinking about standing on the stage and reading my poem.

*What if I stumble over my words?* I thought. *Or worse yet, what if I stumble getting onto the stage? Oh, I'll be fine,* I reassured myself as I walked into the gym.

The DJ was playing the Christmas carol, "Deck the Halls." The first thing I noticed was that, with the lights dimmed, the decorations truly did make the gym look like a white Christmas.

And the second thing I noticed was the dress in the window—on Betsy. I hesitated.

Betsy saw me and looked worried. "My aunt bought the dress for me as a surprise," she said nervously. "When she gave it to me last night, I felt guilty."

81

"Why?" I asked.

"I remembered how much you liked it, and well..." he voice trailed off.

"Betsy, you look *so* pretty," I said. "I'm happy for you."

She smiled, clearly relieved.

Mollie skipped up to us and whirled around in her blu velvet party dress. "My friends the famous poets, let's get th party started!" She did a funny dance to "Deck the Halls which made us laugh.

After dancing and playing games, Mollie, Betsy and I we eating the coconut snowball cupcakes my mom and Jerry ha made. As we complimented* each other on our pretty dresse Mollie hatched a brilliant idea.

Since all three of us had more Christmas parties coming u Mollie suggested that we trade dresses. "That way we'll ead have a 'new' dress to wear."

"A three-way dress swap*!" said Betsy. "That's a gre idea."

We figured out how it would work: Betsy was going to wea Mollie's blue velvet dress. Mollie would wear my dress (Mi Maple's dress). And I would wear Betsy's dress—the dress in th window—to my family's Christmas Eve party!

At 7:15 p.m. the principal stood on the stage and called my name to come up and read my poem. "Please welcome Audrey-Ann, who will be reading her winning poem entitled 'The Best Christmas Gift.'" The audience clapped.

The microphone was positioned for my height. One spotlight was shining on me while the rest of the stage was dark.

I looked into the audience and saw my classmates and students from other grades, too. Mr. Skippington, who was wearing a tie with a giant candy cane on it, was sitting at a table with a few other teachers.

Just like I had practiced for my family, I said loud and clear, "Happy holidays, everyone!"

I unfolded the piece of lined notebook paper I'd brought from home. I scanned it. *Help!* There were nine items on this paper, each one with a red check mark next to it.

I panicked*. *This isn't my poem. It's my list of craft supplies!*

# Chapter Twelve

## THE BEST CHRISTMAS GIFT

*Think!* I said to myself. *Try to remember the words to the poem.*

Mr. Skippington came dashing to my rescue. The giant candy cane on his tie was flapping wildly over his shoulder as he leapt from one end of the gym to the other.

He sprinted across the floor, up the stairs, and to the middle of the stage where I was twisting my list as if wringing out a washcloth. He hurriedly handed me a few papers stapled together. "I brought copies of the winning poems," he gasped, out of breath.

"THANKS!" I forgot that I was in front of a microphone, so my voice made an ear-splitting boom. People covered their ears and winced*. I was so startled I jumped back a foot. That got a laugh from the audience. I giggled, too, a little embarrassed.

Mr. Skippington straightened his tie. "Ahem! Let's try this again," he said, bending over to speak into the microphone. "Please welcome Audrey-Ann!"

When the applause quieted down, I began to read:

# The Best Christmas Gift

The best Christmas gift
isn't what you might think.
It's not a diamond necklace
or a bicycle in hot pink.

It's not a fancy vacation,
or a sweater that's oh-so-pretty,
or a wide-screen TV,
or a sweet little kitty.

The gift I have in mind
I won't play with or wear.
It can't sit on my shelf
or decorate my hair.

What will make me happiest
is none of the above.
The present I'll treasure most
is all about love.

This gift will last forever
in my head and in my heart.
It can't be broken or lost.
That's the best part.

While I'm thankful for the presents
that are wrapped beneath my tree,
sharing Christmas with my family
is the best gift to me.

## The End

# Glossary

*Many words have more than one meaning. Here are the definitions of words marked with this symbol \* (an asterisk) as they are used in sentences.*

**ace:** *do very well on a test, get a perfect or nearly perfect grade*

**annual:** *happening every year*

**antsy:** *impatient, restless*

**astonished:** *very surprised*

**buffet, as in "buffet tables":** *tables that hold food so that a gathering of people can help themselves*

**butterflies, as in "butterflies in my stomach":** *a nervous feeling*

**centerpieces:** *decorations placed in the middle of dining tables*

**complimented:** *gave words of approval and praise*

**dead, as in "dead ends":** *roads or paths that come to an end with no place to exit*

**dilly-dallying:** *wasting time for no good reason*

**double-stick:** *sticky on both sides*

**double take:** *a delayed reaction to something unexpected*

**exception, as in "exception to the rule":** *something that does not follow what is usually done*

**festive:** *merry*

**fragile:** *not strong or sturdy*

**glanced:** *looked*

**glimpse:** *a quick look*

**glum:** *sad*

**helium, as in "helium balloons":** *balloons that float*

**inspire:** *cause a creative thought or action*

**maze:** *paths that form a puzzle, making it hard to find one's way through to the end*

**muttered:** *spoke in a low voice or grumbled*

**oodles:** *a great number*

**panicked:** *had a sudden wild fear that is not controlled*

**pizzazz:** *extra special style*

**poke, as in "poke fun at":** *make fun of or tease*

**postpone:** *put off until later*

**reality:** *what is happening in real life*

**skitter:** *move quickly and lightly*

**solo:** *a song performed by one singer*

**stewed:** *thought about troubles, felt anxiety*

**stretcher:** *a table with wheels for carrying an injured or sick person*

**strokes:** *swings, using an object like a club, to hit a ball*

**swap:** *the act of exchanging one object for another*

**tickled:** *very pleased*

**winced:** *showed an uncomfortable feeling by drawing back a bit and twisting the face as if in pain*

# Homemade Gifts Come from the Heart

*Follow Audrey-Ann's lead and make your own creative presents.
Here are a couple of delicious gifts that are good enough to eat.*

## Peppermint Candy Christmas Tree

*This is the centerpiece that Mollie helped make for the
Christmas Celebration. Make it for your holiday table or
for someone special.*

### Supplies you'll need:
Roll of double-stick tape, 9-inch high Styrofoam™ cone (leave
the plastic wrap on to help the tape stick, or wrap it in paper),
3-inch high flowerpot with a hole in the bottom, two bags of
wrapped peppermint candies, heavy paper or foam sheet, small
apple, pencil or chopstick, toothpick, white glue and scissors.

## How to make it:

1. Cover the entire Styrofoam cone with double-stick tape by wrapping strips of tape around the cone. Start at the top and work your way down to the very bottom.

2. Beginning at the top, stick candies on the surface as shown, until the whole cone is covered.

3. Cut a star for the top of the tree from paper or a foam sheet. Trace that star to make a second one. Put one end of a toothpick on the star, add a piece of double-stick tape, and put the second star on top of it. This makes a two-sided star. Poke the other end of the toothpick into the top of the Christmas tree.

4. Set an apple on the table. Cover it with the upside-down flowerpot. Put a pencil or chopstick into the hole of the pot and push the pencil or chopstick straight down (halfway) into the apple. This makes a sturdy "tree trunk."

5. Gently place your tree directly over the "tree trunk" and push down, so the trunk goes straight up and into the middle of the tree. If the trunk is loose in the hole of the Styrofoam, add a few drops of glue on the end of the trunk.

*Remember, craft projects should always be supervised by your parent or a trusted adult.*

92

# Blooming Butterscotch Candy Sunflower

*This blossom makes a great birthday, get-well or thinking-of-you gift that's bright and cheery.*

## Supplies you'll need:

Roll of double-stick tape, circular Styrofoam that measures 5 or 6 inches across (leave the plastic wrap on to help the tape stick, or wrap it in paper), 3-inch high flowerpot, two bags of wrapped butterscotch candies, two large pieces of heavy paper or two foam sheets, small apple, pencil or chopstick, toothpick, white glue and scissors.

## How to make it:

1. Cover the entire piece of circular Styrofoam with double-stick tape.

2. Cut a petal shape out of the paper or foam sheet. Trace it and cut enough petals to go around the circle on the front and back. Stick petals around the edges on the front half of the circle.

3. Stick candies on the front surface as shown, until it is covered. Turn it over.

4. Repeat steps 1 through 3 to cover the back of the Styrofoam circle, alternating petals as shown.

5. Set an apple in the flowerpot. Put a pencil or chopstick straight down halfway into the apple. This makes a sturdy "stem" for the flower.

6. Place your sunflower directly over the "stem" and carefully push down, so the stem goes straight up into the bloom. If the stem is loose in the hole of the Styrofoam, add a few drops of glue on the end of the stem. Add loose candies into the top of the flowerpot to cover the apple.

*Remember, craft projects should always be supervised by your parent or a trusted adult.*

## About the Author

Susan Cappadonia Love lives in Milton, Massachusetts with her husband, Scott, and daughters, Sophie and Olivia.

In addition to **The Dress in the Window,** she has also written six other books in the Our Generation® Series, **The Jukebox Babysitters, The Sweet Shoppe Mystery, The Mystery of the Vanishing Coin, Stars in Your Eyes, One Smart Cookie** and **The Most Fantabulous Pajama Party Ever,** as well as other children's books.

Much gratitude goes to the wonderful team of people at Maison Joseph Battat Ltd., including Joe Battat, Dany Battat, Alison Morin, Batia Tarrab, Natalie Cohen, Loredana Ramacieri, Karen Erlichman and Lisa Skolnick. Many thanks to Joanne Burke Casey, Mylene Vallee, Kim Cleland, Julie Kassabian, Emilie Fandrich, Kate Annantuonio and Pam Shrimpton.